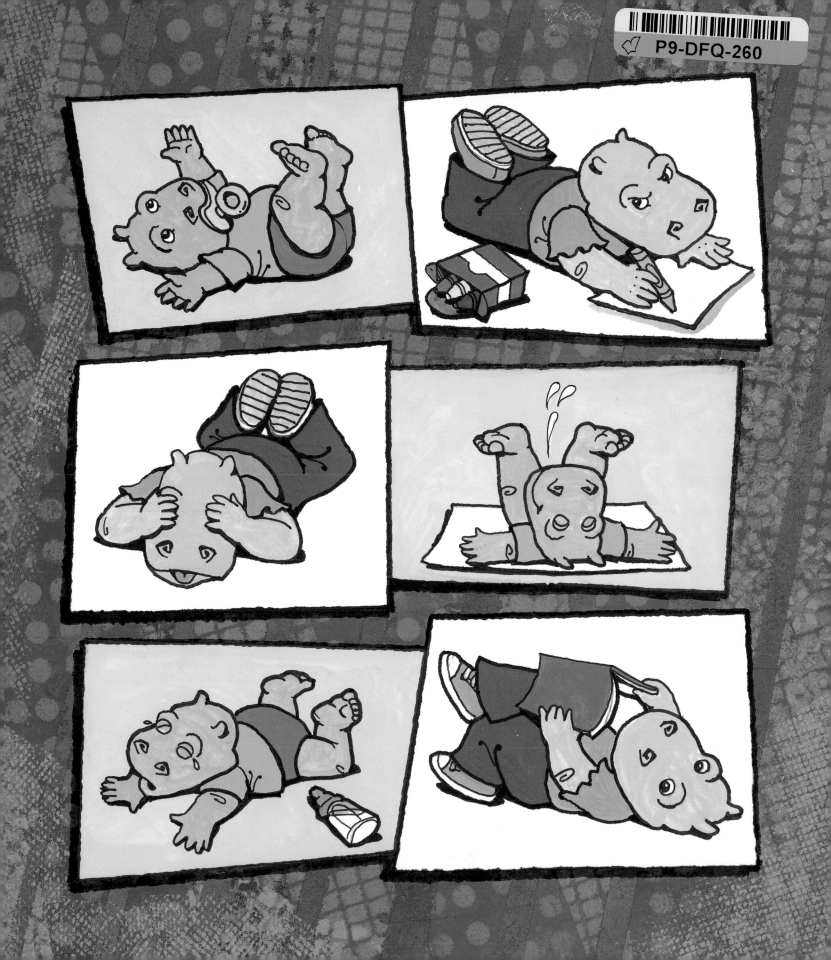

Shirley's Wonderful Baby

BY VALISKA GREGORY

ILLUSTRATED BY BRUCE DEGEN

HARPERCOLLINS*PUBLISHERS*

The unusual textures and patterns in the illustrations were created by applying gouache over hand-cut stencils, plastic and wire meshes, masking tape, and punched-out patterns found in an old industrial plastics warehouse. The illustrations were then finished with pen and ink.

Shirley's Wonderful Baby   Text copyright © 2002 by Valiska Gregory   Illustrations copyright © 2002 by Bruce Degen
Printed in Hong Kong. All rights reserved. www.harperchildrens.com

Library of Congress Cataloging-in-Publication Data
Gregory, Valiska.
   Shirley's wonderful baby / by Valiska Gregory ; illustrated by Bruce Degen.
      p.   cm.
   Summary: Shirley doesn't share her family's sentiment that their new baby is wonderful until Ms. Mump, the baby-sitter,
comes to visit.
   ISBN 0-06-028132-4 — ISBN 0-06-028574-5 (lib. bdg.)
   [1. Babies—Fiction.   2. Babysitters—Fiction.   3. Brothers and sisters—Fiction.]   I. Degen, Bruce, ill.   II. Title.
PZ7.G8624Sh   2002   99-11751
[E]—de21   CIP
                                                                                                                              AC

Typography by Al Cetta   1   2   3   4   5   6   7   8   9   10   ❖   First Edition

For Shirley and her grandchildren,
who are all (especially Shirley) wonderful.
—V.G.

In memory of my big sister, Elaine.
—B.D.

THE trouble with Shirley's new baby brother was that everything Stanley did was wonderful.

When Shirley's father changed Stanley's diaper, the
baby stuck both legs straight up in the air. "Isn't he
wonderful?" said her father.

"What I want to know," Shirley thought, "is just
what's so wonderful about a baby with legs like a turkey?"

"He's wrinkling his tiny nose," said Shirley's
mother. "Isn't he wonderful?"

Shirley rolled her eyes. "How can a baby who
looks like a prune be wonderful?" she thought.
But she didn't say anything at all.

When they took Stanley for a walk, their neighbor tickled the baby under his chin.

"Gaaah," said the baby in a sweet little voice.

"How wonderful!" said the neighbor. "He's a real talker."

"Right," thought Shirley. "If you don't mind a lot of drool and not being able to understand a single word he says."

When they shopped at the grocery store, Shirley had to carry the bag with Stanley's diapers and powder and toys.

"Wonderful," thought Shirley. "He rides. I walk."

And when Stanley dropped his slimy pacifier on the floor, it was Shirley who had to wash it off.

"Wonderful," thought Shirley. "He spits. I rinse."

One day Shirley said to her parents quite casually, "Don't you think it's about time to take this baby back?"

"Why, Shirley," said her mother, "Stanley's a wonderful baby. You'll see."

But when the new baby-sitter arrived, Shirley's father took Ms. Mump right past Shirley's room and showed her Stanley's room first.

"Try not to wake the baby, Shirley," he whispered. "We'll be back soon."

"I hope you know that babies aren't nearly as interesting as everybody thinks they are," said Shirley hopefully.

"Of course I do," said the baby-sitter. "My name is Ms. Mump, and I like my tea with two lumps of sugar and NO babies."

Shirley knew right away that she was going to like the new baby-sitter a lot.

All afternoon she and Ms. Mump played together. They read books, did puzzles, and slurped root beer in the kitchen.

"Your cookies are simply *wonderful,* my dear," said Ms. Mump.

Shirley put on her tap shoes, and Ms. Mump played the piano.

"My dear," said Ms. Mump, "you are the most wonderful tap dancer I have ever seen."

Shirley did a hop-shuffle-step better than she had ever done it before—

But then they both heard Stanley.

"Oops," said Ms. Mump. "Babies are notorious for waking up."

When Stanley saw Ms. Mump, his lower lip started to quiver.

"Sometimes he gets worried about strangers," explained Shirley, "and his diaper is probably wet."

"Revolting," said Ms. Mump. "You'll have to change it, of course."

"Me?" asked Shirley.

"Definitely," said Ms. Mump. She showed Shirley how to sprinkle powder on the baby's bottom and fasten the Velcro strips. Stanley smiled as Shirley tickled his tummy.

"Babies are notorious for smiling," said Ms. Mump.

"Well," said Shirley, "for a baby, he probably smiles pretty good."

Ms. Mump carried Stanley into the living room. "Babies are notorious for being hungry," she said. "You'll have to feed it, of course."

"I get to feed the baby?" asked Shirley.

"Definitely," said Ms. Mump. She lifted Stanley into Shirley's lap, and he made gurgly noises as he drank from his bottle.

"Revolting," said Ms. Mump.

Stanley reached up and patted Shirley's cheek.

"Well," said Shirley, "I guess even babies have to eat."

Ms. Mump put a cloth diaper on Shirley's shoulder.

"Babies are notorious for burping," said Ms. Mump.

She showed Shirley how to hold Stanley and pat his back until he gave a loud burp.

"Revolting," said Ms. Mump.

Stanley nestled his head on Shirley's shoulder.

"Well," said Shirley, "I happen to know that for a baby it was a very good burp."

Ms. Mump put Stanley on a blanket on the
floor.

"Babies are notorious for getting into trouble,"
said Ms. Mump. "Please make sure he doesn't
wander off."

She settled herself in the blue chair with
a thick book.

Shirley wasn't sure what to do next.
"Okay, baby," she said finally, "I'll sing you
a song." Shirley sang "Rock-a-bye, Baby"
three times all the way through, but Stanley
didn't look one bit sleepy.

Shirley gave the baby's rattle a shake, then wrapped his fingers around the handle. Stanley got so excited, he bonked himself on the head, and his lower lip began to quiver again.

"Don't cry, baby," Shirley said, and she kissed him on the forehead.

"Revolting," said Ms. Mump. "Babies don't know very much, do they?"

Stanley reached out and held on to Shirley's thumb.

"Well," said Shirley, "I could probably teach him."

"Now watch this, baby," Shirley said. She hid her face behind her hands.

"Peek-a-boo!" she said as she took her hands away, and the baby grinned. Shirley had to do it over and over again, and then she read Stanley all the old baby books she knew by heart.

"Revolting," said Ms. Mump. "Babies are notorious for wanting attention."

"But Stanley needs attention," said Shirley. "He's just a baby."

"Of course," said Ms. Mump. "How clever of you to think of it, my dear."

When Shirley's parents came home,
Shirley told them how she had changed
Stanley's diaper and burped him and
read him all her baby books.

"Why, Shirley," they said, "that's
wonderful!"

"Babies are notorious for needing their
sisters," said Ms. Mump, "and as a sister,
your Shirley is wonderful."

Shirley smiled and gave Stanley a hug.

"Gaaah," said Shirley's baby, because he knew Shirley was wonderful all along.

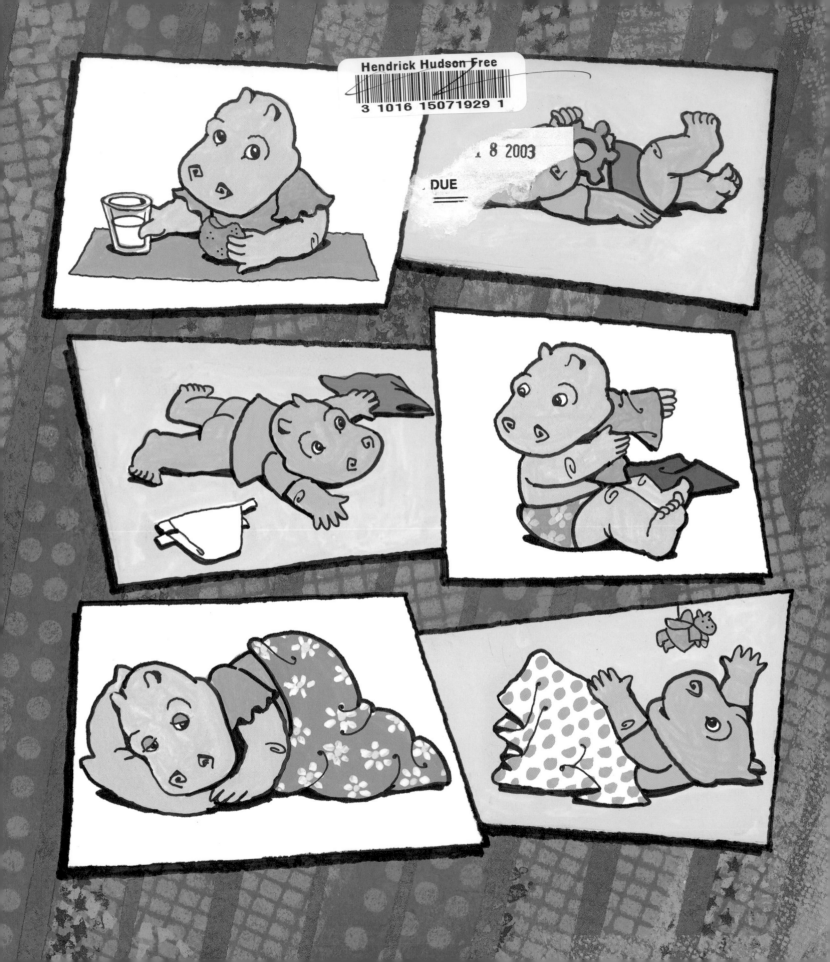